DUCK AND DUKES

by

The Rev. W. Awdry

with illustrations by
Gunvor & Peter Edwards

Grolier

Crosspatch

SKARLOEY made a face. "Not again, Nancy, *please*."

"Just a teeny polish," she coaxed. "You must look nice for your 100th birthday."

"I *am* nice. You're just a fusspot."

"And you're a horrid old crosspatch." Nancy polished him vigorously.

Skarloey smiled. "Nancy," he said, "I really was a crosspatch once. Shall I tell you?"

"Yes, please."

"Well, come down. I can't tell it properly while you're fussing up there."

"Just five minutes then; no longer." Nancy sat down on a box, and the old engine began.

"Talyllyn, Dolgoch, Rheneas and I, were built together in England."

"Who," asked Nancy, "are Talyllyn and Dolgoch?"

"Talyllyn is my twin; Dolgoch is Rheneas'. Their Railway is at Towyn in Wales, and they're 100 too. They were green, and we were red. Talyllyn and I had four wheels then, and no cab. We thought we were wonderful, and talked about how splendid we'd look pulling coaches."

"What about trucks?" asked Nancy.

Skarloey chuckled. "We had no use for *them*," he said.

"I was finished first, and sent away on a ship. I didn't like that. It wobbled dreadfully. At the Port the Big Railway kept me waiting. They had no cranes to lift me out. It wasn't the Fat Controller's Railway then. He would have managed much better."

"What did they do?" asked Nancy.

"They used the ship's derricks. They nearly turned me upside down," said Skarloey indignantly, "and left me hanging while they arranged the truck."

"You must have looked funny," gurgled Nancy.

"Yes and I felt it too! I got crosser and crosser.

"They fastened me to the truck at last, and an engine took me away. His name was Neil— he was ugly but kind, and we were soon friends.

" 'So ye're bound for the Wee Railway,' he said. 'Ye must put some order into those trucks. The havers they make, ye'd hairdly believe.'

"I didn't like the sound of that. But I was too tired to say anything.

"Plenty of people were waiting when we got there, but they weren't used to engines, and it was dark before I was on my rails.

"Then they left me, lonely and unhappy, and wishing Rheneas would come.

"Trucks were everywhere next morning. Suddenly, with a rattle and a roar, a train of loaded ones came in. I was surprised. 'There's no engine!' I said.

"A workman laughed. 'They've come down by gravity,' he said. 'The empty ones need pulling up, though. That's why *you've* come.'

" 'But can't they go up by gra-whatever-it-was-you-said?'

" 'Gravity only brings things down. We need horses, or engines like you to pull them up.'

" 'What! Have *I* to pull *trucks*?'

" 'Of course.'

" 'I won't! I want coaches.'

"He just laughed and walked away.

"Soon, Mr Mack, the Manager, arrived with some men. He showed them my parts from a book. 'We're going to steam you, Skarloey,' he said.

" 'Can I pull coaches, Sir?'

" 'No, certainly not!'

"I gave him such a look! They didn't understand engines, so it was easy! My fire wouldn't burn, and I made no steam. I just blew smoke at them! They called me bad names, but I didn't care.

"Next day they tried again, and the next, and the next. I just gave them my Look, and wouldn't do a thing!

"At last the Manager said, 'Very well, *be* a crosspatch; but we're not going to look at your sulky face all day. We'll cover you up and leave you till you're a better engine.'

"They did, too," chuckled Skarloey. "They fetched a big tarpaulin, and covered me right up. I didn't like that at all!"

"I think it served you right," said Nancy severely.

"Never mind her, Skarloey. Please tell us what happened next."

Nancy turned in surprise. A group of people had quietly come up to listen while Skarloey was telling her his story.

Duck and Dukes

". . . BUT I keep telling you," said Duck. "There *are* no Dukes. They were fine and stately, but they've all been scrapped."

Peter Sam goggled in horror. "This is dreadful," he wailed. "The Thin Controller said the Owner said the Duke said he was coming to our Centenary to open our extension round the lake, and now he's scrapped and Skarloey's and Rheneas' birthday will be spoilt. Oh dear! Oh dear!"

He bustled away with his empty coaches to tell his bad news.

"I think," said Skarloey, "that Duck was pulling your wheels."

"No, Skarloey, he was quite serious."

"He always jokes like that," chuckled Skarloey, but no one agreed, and they argued so loudly that the Thin Controller came to stop their noise. They told him about Duck, but he paid no attention. "I've no time for his nonsense now," he snapped. "There's a change in tomorrow's work. Skarloey, you will meet the Duke at 11.0 instead of 10.30." And he hurried away.

"If there *is* a Duke," said Duncan, but they were all too tired to argue any more.

They spent a gloomy night, but cheered up next morning when the cleaners greeted the birthday engines with an "All-metal Band". Drivers and Firemen joined in, and even the Thin Controller banged a metal plate as loudly as anyone. The engines punctuated the "music" with their whistles.

The Owner laughed and held his ears. Presently he looked at his watch. "That's enough," he ordered, so Rusty, Sir Handel and Duncan went at once to find their coaches.

Visitors crowded the Big Station. They wanted to go to places along the line to watch the celebrations.

Peter Sam and Rheneas had carefully practised their parts. Passengers in Agnes, Ruth, Lucy, Jemima and Beatrice all wore clothes of 1865. Rheneas had to pull them behind Peter Sam's Television train, not too close and not too far away, so that the cameramen could take their pictures.

Visitors waved as they went by, and at last they reached the special sidings near the extension, where they settled down to wait. "Listen!" said Peter Sam at last. "Here's Skarloey; they're cheering him."

"Good!" answered Rheneas. "Perhaps that will make up for his disappointment over the Duke."

Skarloey wasn't disappointed at all. "I've brought the Duke! I've brought the Duke! I've brought the Duke!" he puffed, and triumphantly came to stand between the two trains.

A distinguished-looking man stepped out, climbed to Skarloey's footplate, and drove him on the new line round the lake and back again. Then, standing on Skarloey's front bufferbeam, he said, "Ladies, Gentlemen, and Engines, I have pleasure in declaring your lovely lakeside loopline now open. . . ."

Peter Sam could bear it no longer. "Excuse me, Sir Duke," he burst out. "Are you real?"

There was shocked silence.

The Duke smiled. "Skarloey said you'd been listening to Duck," he answered. "Duck thinks Dukes were Great Western Engines, but Dukes are really people. I am happy to assure you, Peter Sam, that I am a real live Duke."

"I'll give Duck 'Dukes'!" muttered Peter Sam, but he was sternly hushed!

The Duke turned to the Owner. "I congratulate you, Sir, on your remarkable Railway. It must be a record indeed to have two locomotives in regular service, and both a hundred years old. Long life, then, and good running to Skarloey and Rheneas, your famous old engines." The cheering and clapping died away. "Speech!"

shouted someone, and the cry was taken up. "Go on, Rheneas," whispered the Owner, so rather nervously the old engine began.

"Thank you, your Grace, and everyone, for your kind wishes. You've given us both a lovely 100th birthday; but, your Grace, Skarloey and I aren't the only 'record' engines. We've got twin brothers. Talyllyn and Dolgoch were built at the same time as us, so they are 100 too, *and* they're still at work. Their Railway's at Towyn, in Wales. Please go and see them, your Grace, and everybody, and wish them Many Happy Returns from Skarloey and Rheneas, their 'Little Old Twins'."